BATTLE BUGS

BUGS

THE POISON FROG ASSAULT

by JACK PATTON
illustrated by BRETT BEAN

With special thanks to Adrian Bott

Text copyright © 2015 by Hothouse Fiction
Cover and interior art by Brett Bean, copyright © 2015 Scholastic Inc.

All rights reserved. Published by Scholastic Inc., *Publishers since 1920*, 557 Broadway, New York, NY 10012, by arrangement with Hothouse Fiction. Series created by Hothouse Fiction.

ISBN 978-0-545-70744-2

10 9 8 7 6 5 4 3 2 1   15 16 17 18 19

Printed in the U.S.A.   40
First printing 2015
Book design by Phil Falco and Ellen Duda

CONTENTS

GAME ON

On the basketball court at Burgdale Elementary, the tension was running high. Burgdale was playing Green Park, a local rival. Both schools had plenty of fans cheering them on and chanting at each other across the court. The score was tied at 24, with a couple of minutes left.

At the top of the key, Max Darwin watched eagerly for a chance to score.

He caught the eye of Green Park's captain. The tall boy smirked at him. "Go get changed, Darwin!" he yelled. "The game's in the bag."

Max gritted his teeth and stared right back. "It's tied with five minutes on the clock. I don't call that 'in the bag.'"

Burgdale *couldn't* lose today . . . not to Green Park, of all schools! There was more at stake here than just a game. Last year, Green Park had humiliated Burgdale with a 32–6 defeat. Max had missed a few baskets and blamed himself for the loss. Today, he was going to make up for that.

A Green Park player threw the ball in, but a Burgdale guard intercepted it and started to dribble, looking for someone who was in the clear.

Max held up his hands; his teammate quickly threw him the ball, and Max pivoted toward the basket.

Now was his chance! None of the Green Park players were near the hoop. He had a clear shot.

"Go, Max, go!" screamed someone from the bleachers.

Max hesitated. It was a long shot from where he was standing—maybe *too* long. He was a good player, but it was risky to shoot from so far away.

Max made up his mind. *Better play it safe*, he thought, dropping the ball back down. A little closer and he could go in for the layup.

Dribbling quickly, Max dodged past two Green Park guards as he made for the hoop. It was right in front of him now. He couldn't miss. He took the shot—but out of nowhere, the Green Park captain appeared and slammed the ball out of the air, away from the basket. In the next second, he slammed into Max, who went flying.

Max fell hard on his butt. "Ow!"

"Aww, I'm sorry, Darwin," cooed the Green Park captain. "Did I wreck your shot?"

He held out a hand as if to help Max up, but Max knew he'd just snatch it away and laugh if Max tried to take it. He got up on his own.

"Foul!" shouted the Burgdale fans, but the referee didn't seem to notice.

"Time out!" roared Coach Baker.

The Green Park players rolled their eyes and sneered.

The Burgdale team gathered around Coach Baker. He put his hands on his hips. Max looked down at his sneakers. He'd been so close to glory.

"The ref must be blind!" said the coach. "But we can't just hand them this game on a plate, right?"

"No, Coach," came a few mumbles.

"You gonna lose your nerve, just when it counts the most?"

"No, Coach." A little louder this time.

"I can't hear you."

"No, COACH!" they thundered back.

"That's better." The coach leaned in close. "Let me tell you somethin' important that holds true on and off the court. Are you listening, Max?"

Max looked up into the coach's serious brown eyes. "Yes, Coach."

"Good. Listen up and repeat after me: *Sometimes you gotta take a long shot, 'cause it's the only shot you got!*"

Max knew those words were meant for him, but the coach was making the whole team say it so he wouldn't feel bad.

As he repeated the words, he flinched. Something was tickling his arm. He went to brush it away but stopped and looked instead.

An ant! It must have climbed onto him when he was knocked to the hardwood. It looked like it was waving its forelegs at him.

"So, you ready to fight? Are you ready to win? Are you ready to go back out there and beat Green Park?" Coach Baker yelled.

"Yes, COACH!" the team yelled back.

Max glanced down at his feet. There was another ant, crawling on his sneaker. He knelt down and pretended to tie his lace so he could get a better look.

Bug Island came rushing into his mind. Even the excitement of a basketball game couldn't compare to the adventures he'd had there. As special adviser to the heroic bug forces of the Battle Bugs, he'd helped them out against their lizard foes twice before. Last time, he and the Battle Bugs had defended a mountain pass against collared lizards, cleverly using the talents of golden orb weavers, bombardier beetles, and termites. Before that, he'd helped some army ants make a bridge to evacuate bugs that were in danger.

Even though it was terrible timing, Max knew what the sight of this ant outside of its natural habitat must mean: The bugs needed his help!

Max quickly thought of a plan. Maybe if he slipped away now, he'd still be back in time to beat those Green Parkers.

"Coach?" he said quickly. "Can I use the bathroom?"

Coach Baker sighed and looked at his watch. "Make it quick."

As Max ran to the locker room, he could hear the Green Park team laughing. Max shook his head. He'd be back to deal with them soon. But right now he had bigger things on his mind.

The locker room was empty, so Max pulled out *The Complete Encyclopedia of Arthropods* from his bag. The huge leather-bound book was glowing softly around the edges. So the Battle Bugs did need his help! It must be time for another adventure.

Time moved slowly in the real world when Max was on Bug Island, but he knew

he'd still have to be quick, or he'd miss the end of the game . . . and that would be a disaster he'd never live down.

As Max opened the book and pulled out the magnifying glass, he could just make out a stream of ants. They were moving in a long column. The bugs were on the march. But why? And where?

It looked like he was about to find out. The book's pages loomed up at him, growing huge as a brick wall, as Max shrank down to bug size. He began to spin like a swimmer caught in a whirlpool. He was headed to Bug Island once more!

ROAD TO BATTLE

Max landed with a bump on something that looked like a long, green diving board with a pointy tip. It wobbled underneath him.

He hung on tight and tried to figure out where he was. It took him a second to realize he was hanging on to a single blade of grass. Being shrunk down to bug size wasn't easy to get used to, no matter how many times he did it.

He stood up carefully. In the distance loomed the edges of a jungle. For once, Max had ended up in a clearing and had a good view of his surroundings. The other times he'd landed on Bug Island, he'd found giant flowers or trees towering over him, but not now.

Max couldn't tell where exactly he was, but it was lush and green and hot. He hadn't fallen into Reptile Island by mistake— thank goodness. According to the bugs, that place had sand and rocks all over it.

Close by, the grass changed to bare earth. It appeared to be a path of some kind, leading off in both directions as far as Max could see. By the look of it, many bugs had trampled it down over the years. A main road, for sure. But where did it lead?

Max peered into the distance. He could see Fang Mountain rising above the jungle. The crafty lizards had once tried to find a way through a mountain pass there, but Max had managed to block their way with a rockfall.

There was always some new danger coming from Reptile Island. For many years, Bug Island had been separate from Reptile Island, cut off by the sea. Bugs of all different kinds had lived together in peace, safe from lizard predators. Then one day, a volcano erupted. The lava that flooded down to the sea cooled into rock and formed a land bridge. Now the two islands were joined, and the bugs were under constant attack from the lizards.

When the bugs were in desperate need of help, they turned to Max. But where was the danger this time? He couldn't see anything but grass for miles around.

"Where are you, bugs?" Max said to himself.

Right on cue, he heard a droning noise, faint and far away, but coming closer.

"Buzz!" he yelled, leaping to his feet and setting the blade of grass boinging up and down again. He waved, hoping his friend was on the way. Buzz, the hornet, was the flight commander of the Battle Bugs.

Riding on her back, high above the island, was always a thrill. Max couldn't wait.

But it wasn't Buzz at all. The drone grew louder and louder until it was deafening. A black cloud had appeared in the distance, and now it came rushing toward Max, hovering just above the ground.

Max could see now that it was a huge swarm of flies coming his way, and they weren't slowing down. Max watched them grow closer and closer. Then he remembered that every single fly in that swarm was as big as he was. In seconds, it would be like standing in the middle of a busy highway. He had to get out of the way!

Max lowered himself to the ground and started running. But it was too late. The drone had grown to a roar now. The first of the flies flew past in a rush of wind, a blue-bottle as big as a bull. Then the swarm hit.

He was caught up in a black snow-storm of huge, buzzing bodies. One of them knocked him flat on his back. He looked up and caught flashes of domed eyes, blurry wings, and wobbling mouthparts flashing past too fast to see.

He tried to stand. "It's me!" he yelled. "It's Max! General Barton's friend!" But none of the flies seemed to hear. They buzzed past him, swerving this way and that in total chaos.

Then, just as suddenly as it had come, the swarm passed by. Max watched the cloud move off down the road.

"What in the world was that about?" he said out loud.

At least he was in the clear now. Or so he thought.

Beneath his feet, the ground trembled. "NOW what?" Max groaned.

The sound grew louder until Max was certain what it was—the dull, thudding footsteps of *a lot* of bugs. Suddenly the flies' charge made sense. They had been scouting ahead of whatever was coming now . . .

Max saw them crashing through the grass, tall green bugs with bulbous eyes and V-shaped heads, their powerful legs bending the blades back as they marched. There was no mistaking their clawed, folded forelimbs, which they whipped out in front of them to the rhythm of the march. Praying mantises—hundreds of them!

Max had hoped to run off the road and wait until they passed by, but there was no avoiding the mantises. They marched in formation, chanting a gruff song as they stomped toward him:

"Fight! Fight! Claw, claw, bite!

Reptiles, reptiles, we will smite!

Beat them back with mantis might!

Claw! Bite! Fight, fight, FIGHT!"

They thundered over Max, paying no attention to him at all. Max ran desperately between their legs, helplessly caught in the stampede. He shouted for them to watch where they were going and that he was a friend, but the mantises just kept singing their marching song. They either couldn't hear him, or didn't care.

A mantis leg whacked him, hard as a tree branch, and flung him back through the air.

"Get out of the way," the mantis roared, marching ahead as if nothing had happened. Max tripped into the next bug, and in a terrible moment he knew those snapping forelegs would slice him in half unless he did something.

He quickly curled into a ball like a wood louse, pulling his arms and legs in, and the mantis claws whipped past so close he could feel the breeze.

Max tumbled down to the ground, rolled, and got up. As the last of the mantises passed by, he looked down the path to see what could be coming next. The way his luck was going so far, it would be a tidal wave of ants!

But to his delight, he heard a familiar voice calling his name. "Hey! Max! Hooman bean! Is that you?"

"Spike!" he yelled in relief. "Am I glad to see you!"

Spike, the emperor scorpion, came lumbering up. "Good to see you, too. Hop on!"

Max gratefully climbed onto Spike's smooth armor-plated back. He felt a *lot* safer now. "What's going on?" he asked. "I was almost killed twice in the last five minutes!"

"The Battle Bugs are on the march," Spike said proudly. "We're going to war."

"Is it the lizards? Are they back?"

"It's the lizards, all right," Spike said, sounding furious. "We've had word from the underground bug resistance—"

"Underground?" Max interrupted.

"Yes. It's a network of bugs that use underground tunnels to run supplies and carry messages. They told us that a whole lizard battalion is based on the Pincer Plains."

"So that's why you need my help!"

Spike nodded. "This is a big one, Max. General Barton needs your brain!"

RAPID RESPONSE

Now that he was safe on Spike's back, Max could relax a little and take in the amazing sight of the bug march. The insects and arachnids trooped along in a snaking column that wound along the path far out of sight in each direction. Spike scuttled along past the praying mantises, who marched in step and kept up their deadly-looking, claw-snapping chant.

Something, somewhere was busy keeping them in rhythm with a shrill marching beat. It made a high-pitched SKREE-SKREE noise until Max had to stuff his fingers in his ears.

"What *is* that?" he asked Spike.

"The cicadas!" Spike told him. "Over there on the left, marching behind the orb weaver spiders. Isn't it stirring?"

"That's one word for it," Max yelled. He took a good look at the cicada brigade. They were fat, bulbous insects with long wings and bulging eyes. Their sound seemed too loud to come from something so small, but the beat managed to keep all the other insects in line.

"HALT!" came a cry from far ahead. The bugs passed the word to one another down the line, from ladybug to water boatman to cricket to centipede, all the way through the ranks until it reached Spike and Max: "Halt! Go no farther for now."

The battalions came to a stop. Immediately, many of the bugs began to groom themselves, rubbing their legs together or whirring their wings.

Max stood up on Spike's back. "What is it? An attack?"

Moments later, another command came buzzing down the line: "All bugs to hold position until fly scouts report back. NO, repeat, NO attacks to be made without permission. Special adviser Max, please report to General Barton immediately."

"Where's Barton?" Max asked.

"He's right up at the front, leading the march," said Spike. "Don't worry, I'll have us there in a sec."

So the flies hadn't been at the front of the march at all. They'd just been the first bugs Max had seen.

Max and Spike made their way through the crowd to the very front of the line, where a surly-looking ring of stag beetles stood facing outward, forming a defensive line.

"Stop right there!" one of the stag beetles roared. "Nobody reaches the general without authorization!"

"At ease, soldier," came Barton's deep voice from inside the ring. Max could see the enormous titan beetle's head looming above his bodyguards. "Max is a friend. Let them through."

To Max's delight, it wasn't just Barton waiting for him. Buzz, the hornet, and Webster, the trap-door spider, were here already, too. Buzz greeted him with a cheery "Hey there!" and Webster squeaked "Hello!" shyly and shuffled backward.

Standing in Barton's shadow was an insect Max had never met before. He was a winged beetle about Buzz's size, with antennae that twitched eagerly as if he were tuning in to a radio signal. Max was startled to see a faint glow coming from his abdomen. That identified him at once. This bug was a firefly!

"Welcome back to Bug Island, Max," Barton rumbled. "Glad to see you made it here in one piece."

Max thought of the slicing mantis claws that had nearly cut him to bits but decided not to mention it. "Happy to help, General. What's up?"

"I'll explain. First, let me introduce you to Glower, the leader of the underground resistance."

The firefly stepped forward. "I'm more of a manager than a leader, really," he said modestly. "The resistance is a team effort."

Max liked the quiet, polite insect immediately. "Glad to meet you, Glower."

"Likewise, Max. I've heard a lot about your brains."

"Glower and his staff of fireflies and glowworms have a very important job," explained Barton. "They pass intelligence to our troops from their spy stations."

"How?" Max asked curiously. The firefly didn't look very strong or fast, so why would he be a messenger? It didn't seem to make sense.

"With signals," said Glower. "Fireflies like me can use our glowing bodies to signal to one another. We flash in special patterns that only we can understand."

"A team of fireflies can flash a message from one side of Bug Island to the other in less than a minute," Barton said proudly.

Max's mouth fell open. "That's incredible!" It was just like how spies in the human world used to signal to one another, using Morse code or secret messaging symbols.

"One of our lookout posts reports that General Komodo is massing his troops on the Pincer Plains," Glower went on. "The lizards have been pouring across the lava bridge."

"Luckily, thanks to the underground resistance, we have a chance to hit them first. Rapid response. Pow!" Buzz added, her wings beating enthusiastically.

"That's why we're mar-marching," stammered Webster. "I wanted to stay in my burrow, but they said I wasn't allowed."

"Fresh air will do you good," Buzz said, giving Webster a cheery poke with her foreleg. Webster made a "meep" noise and curled his legs up.

"So we're making a surprise attack?" Max asked excitedly. If they were lucky, this could be the blow that finished Komodo once and for all! "Which troops are you sending in first?"

Barton looked ahead to where the Pincer Plains lay flat in the distance. "So far, we only know the size of the Lizard Army, not its composition. We need to figure out what we're up against."

Max nodded. "So let's send a scouting party. Buzz can—"

"It's already done," Barton interrupted. "I've sent the flies ahead as advance scouts. They can get in close and see what sort of lizards Komodo is throwing at us. Then I'll know which troops to use."

Max and Buzz glanced at each other. Max knew they were both thinking the same thing. "Flies? But surely the hornets are tougher?" Max said.

"Ah, but we have a lot more flies than hornets!" Barton snapped his pincers impatiently. "Besides, lizards can't fly. What danger could they be to any airborne bug?"

"I guess," said Max, feeling worried.

"I'm confident the new troops will be able to deal with any threat. You should see the new mantis and cicada battalions!"

"I already have," Max said darkly. "One of the mantises nearly hacked me to pieces!"

"Oh," said Barton. "That is . . . regrettable."

"It's okay. It was an accident," Max replied.

"Once we know what we're dealing with, I want your help to plan an attack," Barton said. "Those brains of yours haven't let us down yet!"

There was nothing to do but wait, nervously, for the fly scouts to report back. Max chatted with Buzz and Webster to pass the time, while Glower retreated into the shadows. The firefly seemed to be most comfortable in the dark.

From time to time, the bugs glanced up into the blue, silent sky. Nothing showed.

"Blast it," Barton finally snapped. "Where *are* those flies?"

"Ran into something they couldn't handle, I bet," said Buzz quietly.

Barton ignored the hornet. "Max, would you and Spike scout ahead? See what's keeping the flies. And stay out of sight!"

"Roger!"

Max set off on Spike. As they continued down the road, Max wondered what could have delayed the flies: *Frogs, maybe, striking with their long, sticky tongues? Or webs that some careless spider had left behind?*

Then he spotted something up ahead that made him look twice: A fly, buzzing high above.

"Hey, look!" he shouted to Spike. "They're coming back!"

As the lonely fly zipped overhead, he saw a whole group of them in the distance. But Max could tell that something was wrong. The flies weren't moving in unison, as before. They looked disordered and chaotic.

"What's going on?" Max shouted up at the returning flies. But the panicked flies were in too much of a hurry to reply.

Soon, peering into the distance, Max could see for himself. The whole swarm began to tear back along the marching highway. But now, something else stood out clearly against the bright blue sky. Wheeling and dipping, snatching at the flies, red flashes of feathered wings plowed into the flies' ranks.

"Uh-oh." Spike stared in horror. "They look like—"

"Birds!" Max cried.

THREAT FROM ABOVE

"GO, Spike, GO!" Max shouted. "Back to Barton! We need to sound the alarm!"

Max and Spike went charging back to the bug column, yelling as loudly as they could. A horrible thought popped into Max's mind. Many birds preyed on insects. He suddenly realized what must have happened to the unlucky flies.

A panicking fly whizzed past Max's head from behind. Another bounced off Spike, spun away through the air, and had to struggle to fly straight again. The fly scouts were in full retreat, zooming back to the bug column in buzzing chaos.

"So much for our scouts!" Spike grunted, scuttling for all he was worth.

Max looked back over his shoulder. As the first rank of bugs began to react, taking up battle positions, the shrieking birds shot down from the sky. They dived like bomber planes, scattering the flies. There was no mercy in their bright little eyes. Their beaks looked sharp and deadly. Spike turned back too, and gasped in horror.

"Spike, what are those?" Max yelled.

"Specially trained flycatchers, by the look of it. They're worse than the lizards, that crew—I've heard they can catch a million flies each! Million-flycatchers, that's what Buzz calls 'em!"

"*Vermilion* flycatchers," Max corrected him. He'd heard of those. They were bright red, fierce, and fast bug-killers. No doubt they'd snap up a bug-sized boy, too!

The swarm of scout flies was trying to make its way back to the bug column, but the flycatchers kept swooping through it and scattering them. No sooner had they finished one fly-through than they swooped around and headed back for another. The poor flies were no match for the fierce and fast flycatchers.

Barton's ring of bodyguards came into view at the head of the column. Max hung on tight, as Spike put on a fresh burst of speed. "We gotta warn the general!" he huffed.

When they reached Barton, they found he was already barking orders at his troops. "I want bombardier beetles ready to blast anything that comes in range! Mantis soldiers, form a defensive line. If you see anything that's not a bug, rip it out of the sky!"

"General," Max gasped, "we have to ground the flies."

Barton's pincers gaped wide in amazement. "Ground them? But on land they'll be sitting targets."

"Exactly! The flycatchers will dive down after them, bringing them within range of our bug forces!"

"Excellent thinking. Cicadas, signal the flies to land."

As the cicadas blasted out their message and the flies began to drop to ground level, Max made another suggestion: "Some of the flycatchers might not take the bait. So let's send Buzz's hornet squadron to attack the birds in the air."

Barton nodded. "Buzz?"

"I thought you'd never ask," the hornet said, whirring her wings eagerly. "Squadron leaders, follow me. Ready . . . *launch!*"

As the flycatcher birds plunged down, ready to snatch up what they thought were defeated fly foes, the black-and-gold hornet fighters rose as one. Stingers braced and ready, they shot up toward the oncoming birds.

"It's working!" Max yelled. The flycatchers, taken by surprise, swirled and flapped in confusion, squawking in rage, as the hornets bombarded them from all sides. These weren't the helpless, bumbling flies they had scattered moments before. These were vicious, stinging warriors.

A few of the birds, crazy with greed, struggled through the hornet barrage and headed for the remaining flies, who were now trembling on the ground among their fellow bugs. Max grinned to see that the

flycatchers had fallen into his trap. Now they were right where he wanted them.

"Battle Bugs, charge!" he roared, urging Spike into the fight. They charged the flycatchers, leading the bugs into the fray.

Spike slammed his stinger into a fat flycatcher before it could gobble up its target. The bird squawked and turned, flapping up into the air. With Max calling out targets, the scorpion lashed out with his pincers, and other bugs stung the birds until they had to retreat.

Behind Max came the wave of praying mantises, eager to prove themselves in their first real fight. They chanted their battle song—"Claw, Claw, Bite!"—as they raked the birds with their clawed forelegs.

The flycatchers quickly realized they'd been tricked. "Back into the air!" one of them screeched.

Max and the bugs braced themselves for rush after rush of counterattack from the flycatchers. The birds took to the skies, then zoomed down once again, on blindingly fast attack runs, diving at any bugs they could see. Spike stood with his pincers ready, snatching at the birds, as they came hurtling by.

Max hadn't been in a battle as tough as this before. From all around came the calls of birds and the scrabbling sounds of bugs fighting for their lives. The bugs were holding their own, but Max needed to see how Buzz and her squadron were doing.

He swerved Spike out of the action and looked up at the swarming hornets, trying to find Buzz in the dogfight.

But the next moment, a crushing pain gripped his waist and he was yanked off Spike's back and into the air.

"No!" Max cried, as the ground disappeared at breakneck speed. Max looked around and found he was staring right into two beady black eyes.

To his horror, he realized he was in a bird's beak. The flycatcher had blindsided him and snatched him off Spike's back. Any second now he'd be swallowed!

"Get *off* me!" he yelled, elbowing the bird in the face as hard as he could. Startled, the bird dropped him. It had never met a bug that acted like *that* before.

Max fell through the air and landed with a bump, rolling over and over in the dust. Luckily, he was unhurt. But he had no idea where in the bug army he'd landed. Spike was nowhere to be seen, and the bugs here were in total chaos, running around in panic or burrowing into the ground to get away from the fighting.

A dark shadow fell over him. The flycatcher landed right in front of him, raising its wings like a villainous cloak.

"What *are* you?" it asked in a menacing, squawking voice. "Little bug with no armor and no stinger?"

"I'm something you don't want to mess with," Max warned, sounding braver than he felt.

The flycatcher laughed. "You look soft and delicious, like a grub. Let me see how good you taste."

It lunged. Max looked around for anything nearby he could reach, and his fingers wrapped around a stone. With all the force he could manage, he hurled it at the bird, smacking it right in the eye. The bird let out a terrible shriek and beat its wings in a mad flurry, feathers flying everywhere.

Max scrambled away. The battle was turning into a rout. He desperately needed to find cover, fast. There was a tree nearby, but that was no good because the trunk was too smooth to climb. Some shrubs farther away looked like they might offer shelter. He could dive in among their tangled stems and hope for the best.

Max ran for them. From behind came an angry scream and a sound of furious flapping. He looked back. It was the bird, winging after him, sending up clouds of dust. The beak gaped wide. This time, Max knew, it would bite him in half.

He sprinted toward the green shrubs with a sick feeling that he wouldn't make it. His legs ached. He couldn't hope to outrun something that could fly. Max wondered how the basketball game would end, and what his schoolmates would say when he never came back from the locker room.

"Max!" came a shout from the base of the tree. "Over here!"

Max jerked his head around. There was no doubt where the voice was coming from. Its owner was jumping up and down, waving his wings and all his legs, showing Max exactly where to go. It was Glower, the bug resistance leader!

The firefly was half-hopping, half-flittering anxiously around a hole between two of the tree's roots, urging Max on.

Safety! Max thought frantically.

As the bird swept in for the kill, Max dashed for the opening. He pumped his legs as fast as they could go, running for all he was worth. As the bird's beak snapped down, trying to clip his ankles, he gave a final burst of speed and leaped into the darkness.

THE HIVE

Max dived into the hole. The flycatcher's beak whammed down into the dirt only inches behind him.

Glower shoved his body up against a stone that lie beside the opening. He strained with all his legs until the stone rolled across the entrance. It completely closed off the opening, muffling the bird's angry cries.

Max leaned against the wooden walls, gasping for breath. He'd escaped being eaten alive, but now he and Glower were sealed inside the tree in the musty darkness.

"That was close," Max said, breathing hard. "Thanks for your help back there."

"No problem," said Glower. The little bug sounded very calm, despite the chaos.

"What do we do now? It's pitch-black in here," Max continued, barely able to see his hand in front of his face.

"You aren't nocturnal, I guess."

Max sat down on the cool, damp floor. He felt around, wondering if there was a way out, but his fingers clutched nothing but crumbly earth and decayed wood.

"Nope, definitely not nocturnal," he mumbled. "Maybe if we climb up inside the trunk . . ."

"Perhaps this will help?"

A light flared into life right in front of Max. It was so bright he had to shield his eyes. Through his fingers he could see that the glowing thing was a wide, segmented shape with Glower's head and arms poking out the top of it. It took Max a moment to realize that it was Glower's lower body, lit up as bright as a bonfire.

"Wow," he gasped, impressed. "That's some trick, Glower."

"Sometimes, all you need is a little illumination." Glower flew up into the air and hovered there, shedding his glow all around. In that eerie light, Max could clearly see his surroundings. It wasn't just any old hole he'd flung himself into—it was the entrance to a tunnel.

"Did you know this was here?" he asked, amazed.

"Of course!" Glower said. "I am in charge of the underground resistance, after all."

"Spike did say you were *literally* underground. I forgot!"

"There is a network of tunnels under Bug Island, which only a select few know about. We keep our secrets well hidden."

Max turned to the stone blocking the way he'd come. "So let's go and rescue the others! They can use the tunnels to escape—"

"No," Glower quickly interrupted. "We can't risk it. I need you to follow me, right away."

Glower zoomed down into the tunnel, and Max followed. The firefly hung in the air in front of him like a lantern, showing the way.

As he walked, Max was grateful for that bobbing light. Without it, he'd be lost down here in total darkness. There was only a tiny chance he'd be able to grope his way back out again on his own. If he went any farther down, there'd be no chance at all.

The first section of the tunnel had thick tree roots running through it. Max had to clamber over and around them, while Glower's light danced impatiently ahead of him.

Though he was glad to be alive, he couldn't stop thinking about what was still happening on the surface. The bugs had been running in panic, as the birds attacked. What must the bug column look like now?

"Do you think Spike's okay?" he asked Glower.

"He's a strong fighter," Glower said, without turning around. "He can take care of himself. And his venom is enough to make any flycatcher think twice."

"But there were so many of them! And what about Buzz, and Webster, and Barton? Can't we go back to the surface and help?"

"No," Glower said.

"But that bird might be gone by now."

This time, Glower did look back. "Max," he said seriously, "those bugs are my friends, too. I want them safe as much as you do. It's too dangerous to go back to the surface, but we can fight just as well from down here, using our brains."

Max nodded, and hoped Glower was right.

Together, they descended deeper and deeper into the tunnel system. The farther they went, the more elaborate the network became. Passageways led off at angles, into the dark unknown. They picked their way along narrow ridges and through tight crawl spaces where Max had to wiggle like a grub to get through.

In some places, the tunnels were rigged with traps, and Glower had to talk Max through them, showing him where to walk. A lizard intruder would have ended up caught in a mass of sticky web, speared on a spike, or dropped through a false floor to his doom.

"Is it much farther?" Max kept asking.

Always, the answer would come back: "Not far."

Just as Max was wondering if Glower might be a double agent luring him into danger, they turned a corner. What he saw took his breath away.

The tunnel opened out into a huge, cavernous space where snaking roots threaded in and out of the walls like walkways. The whole cavern was lit up like a Christmas tree. The walls, floor, and even the ceiling glowed with hundreds of tiny lights. Where the roots crisscrossed the cavern, lights went marching in a row, like a lit-up billboard or the colored bulbs at a carnival.

Every single glowing spot was a bug.

"Welcome to Covert Ops," said Glower, with just a hint of pride.

It wasn't just fireflies at work here, Max now saw. There were glowworms, too, fireflies in their larval stage, their bodies pulsing and flickering.

"This is our information exchange," Glower said. "We call it the Hive."

"It's fantastic," Max said.

As Glower led him down the sloped cavern sides, Max overheard the bugs whispering to one another, chattering away like old-fashioned typewriters. When they saw their leader approaching, they broke off their conversations to give him a quick salute, then went back to their work.

"Spies from all across the island pass information back here through our relay system," Glower said. "General Barton knows everything that happens on Bug Island. I just wish we could get some agents onto Reptile Island, too. If I had that kind of access . . ."

His voice trailed off. Max followed him through the forest of lights, looking around in awe, until they reached a group of fireflies who were clustered around a leaf as if it were a table.

"My fellow resistance leaders," Glower explained. "Lumens, Pulsar, Phosphor, Shyne, and Gleamer. What's the news from the front?"

"Our forces are scattered after the bird attack," said Lumens, her light flickering. "They're trying to rally, but many are panicking."

"No one saw it coming," added Pulsar. "The flycatchers normally migrate this time of year. They're never usually a threat.

Running into a flock of them before we reached the Lizard Army is like a bad joke."

"Then what are they doing here?" snapped Glower.

"We have no new information," admitted Shyne.

"Then we need to get some, and fast."

A plan quickly came together. Glower ordered a spying mission to the last-known location of the lizard troops, the Pincer Plains. "A bird attack is unfortunate, but they happen," he said. "Right now, it's only a setback. But if we lose the battle with the lizards because of a random flycatcher attack, it becomes a disaster. I will not allow that."

"No, sir," chorused the other fireflies.

"Max? What do you think?"

"We need information," Max said firmly.

"Good. We're agreed. Lumens and Pulsar, you're with us. Everyone else, await further orders. If anything happens to us, you're in charge."

The scouting team set off into the tunnel network, down toward the Pincer Plains. Max wondered whether Glower's agents had been watching him secretly on his previous visits to Bug Island.

"Be on your guard, everyone," Glower warned. "We've had reports of enemy sightings in our own tunnels."

"Reptiles?" Max asked.

"Frogs. Allies of the lizards. General Komodo has claimed part of Bug Island as his own. He must have found the tunnel entrances there."

"There are spies in our tunnels?" asked Pulsar, horrified.

"There are spies everywhere," Glower muttered darkly.

The team made its way through tunnel after twisting tunnel, always on the lookout for enemy spies, until Max felt they must surely be nearing their destination.

Glower seemed to read his thoughts. "We're directly under the Pincer Plains," he said. "Almost at the lookout point."

Max wondered if he was walking right under General Komodo's scaly belly. It gave him a funny feeling.

Shafts of feeble daylight shone down from up ahead. At last, an exit! One by one, Max and the bugs squirmed up out of the hole. It would be good to breathe fresh air again after the damp, earth-smelling air in the tunnels.

But Max clamped his mouth shut when he saw where they'd emerged. In front of them all, the enormous ranks of the Lizard Army spread out in every direction—collared lizards, chameleons, and geckos—as far as the eye could see. The smell from the ugly beasts was foul, and only an umbrella-like growth of white fungi hanging above them hid the bugs from sight.

"Fan out as far as you dare," whispered Glower. "It's time to show everyone what we spies are made of."

Max's heart beat fast, as he crawled on his hands and knees, dodging between the tall blades of grass and the fat mushrooms bursting from the ground. He stealthily made his way to the edge of the sheltering fungi and hid under a large parasol mushroom, just in time to see a lizard's head looming above the grass.

It looked like a skink—one of the greediest bug-devouring lizards there was. Max would have to be careful not to be caught, as the lizard sniffed the air with his tongue.

As Max crept closer, a second, smaller skink waddled across to join the first. Max froze in place, listening carefully. His heart was pounding out of his chest.

"Hope the flycatchers left some for us," said the small skink. "I'm hungry!"

"They better have," grumbled the bigger one. "Komodo promised them as many flies as they could eat if they delayed migration and helped us. The rest of the bugs are ours!"

Suddenly, it all made sense to Max. The flycatcher attack wasn't just bad luck, and it wasn't a coincidence. The fly scouts had been attacked deliberately, to keep the bugs from getting intel on the Lizard Army.

It could mean only one thing. This was an alliance. Komodo's forces and the birds were working together!

TUNNEL TROUBLE

Max crept back to Glower as fast as he dared. He felt a prickly sensation on his back, as if a lizard might spot him at any time and snap him up.

"I've got something!" he whispered to Glower. "It wasn't a random attack—the birds are working with the lizards!"

Glower looked grave. "In that case, we have to get back to Barton. Fast!"

They quickly found the entrance to the tunnel and climbed back down. Max filled Lumens and Pulsar in, as they quickly retraced their steps through the winding, root-filled passages.

Max gritted his teeth. It was going to take ages to reach the general, but what choice did they have? They couldn't go aboveground. This way might be slow, but it was safe.

"We'll need a plan to tackle the lizards and the birds together," Glower said, as they hurried along. "Barton always speaks highly of your brains, Max. What's the plan?"

Max swallowed. "I don't have one yet."

Glower didn't say anything. Max scrambled over the long-decayed skeleton of a fern leaf and tried to think of what they could do. He couldn't let Barton down.

The only sounds in the tunnels were the soft whirr of firefly wings and Max's sneakers thumping on the bare earth. Then, suddenly, from up ahead came a high-pitched buzz almost like a scream, and the stop-start sound of a wing case trying to open . . . and failing.

"Pulsar!" hissed Glower. He, Max, and Lumens hurried to see what had happened and were stopped in their tracks.

Max stared in horror. Pulsar lay on the ground, his light flickering weakly. The firefly was pinned under the webbed fore-foot of a monstrous frog, big enough to block the whole tunnel.

The frog's skin glistened with slime in the light from the fireflies. It had a striking color pattern, with patches of black and neon yellow. There was only one kind of frog that looked like that.

"It's a poison dart frog!" Max cried.

He knew all about the deadly creatures from watching TV documentaries. Poison oozed from their skin. It was so strong that a single touch could be enough to get the toxins into your system. Once that happened, you were in deep trouble.

As if on cue, Pulsar's light dimmed. The frog lifted up its foot, chuckling, so they

all could see the poisonous slime smeared over Pulsar's body. Max stared in horror, as Pulsar struggled to move.

"What have you done?" he cried.

"What we amphibians do best," the frog hissed.

"Here to spy for your lizard masters, are you?" Glower demanded. "You'll learn nothing from us!"

"Spy?" croaked the frog. "I'm no spy. I'm just having a nice walk through my new home, aren't I?"

"Nice walk?" hissed Lumens.

"This bug shouldn't have crossed into lizard territory, should he?" The frog snorted.

"There isn't lizard territory!" Max yelled. "This is *Bug* Island, and it always will be!"

The frog's laugh sounded like foul gas bubbling through mud. "Oh, I think the lizards and birds will change all that *very* soon. In the meantime, you're all trespassing. And I'm going to make you pay."

The frog lunged toward Max. Slimy, webbed forefeet clutched at him. He ducked out of the way just in time, and the frog's forefoot traced a trail of poisonous slime down the tunnel wall.

"Scatter!" Glower yelled.

The three of them shot off down one of the dark tunnels, with the frog springing down the passageway after them.

"We've got to shake it off," Glower said.

"I'll divert him," Lumens said, "and then head back for Pulsar." She swerved violently around a tight corner and down a side tunnel, splitting off from Max and Glower.

Despite her efforts, the poison dart frog kept steadily following Max and Glower. Max sprinted through the dark tunnels, desperately following Glower's greenish light through the twists and turns. He could see that the tunnels were made of crumbly yellow clay, and he didn't recognize them at all.

"This isn't the way we came!" he said, as the frog chased them around yet another corner.

"I know!" Glower said. "Just keep running!"

Max had no idea where he was. They could have been under a lake, for all he knew. He had to hope Glower wasn't fleeing blindly into the dark. He ran on and on, with the frog only a few steps behind, its bright yellow body glowing in the darkness.

Then, without warning, Glower shouted: "Narrow bridge coming up. Don't look down!"

Max felt better that Glower *did* know where they were going after all—but that good feeling vanished the next second. They came out on a ledge over a cavernous space.

The path stopped dead. There was only a crumbling edge where a large root must once have lain, bridging the gap. Beyond lie a chasm so wide and deep that Max couldn't even see the far side, let alone the bottom.

He tried to skid to a halt, but he had been running full tilt, expecting the bridge to be there. He only just managed to catch himself at the edge where the path crumbled into the abyss below. Dirt and stones broke loose and tumbled into the gap—Max couldn't hear them hit the bottom.

"It's gone," stammered Glower. "The lizard spies must have tipped the bridge root into the pit!"

The poison dart frog came waddling slowly up to them. It knew it didn't have to hurry. Max and Glower had nowhere left to run. Even if Glower could fly to safety, he couldn't carry Max.

"Looks like the end of the line for you," it said with a smirk.

LONG SHOT

Max backed up until he was at the edge of the pit. Glower flew out over the drop, shining his brightest light. The frog blinked, but kept coming.

"You'll never win!" Max yelled into the frog's face. "The bug army is too strong. We'll never give up Bug Island to a bunch of lizards and birds!"

To Max's surprise, the frog laughed. "Birds? They aren't taking over the place, just the lizards! The birds are brave enough when they're up against a few measly flies, but the minute there's any real trouble, they get scared and off they rocket. They're only doing the lizards' dirty work!" The frog licked its glistening lips. "Hold still, now."

With that, the poison dart frog crouched low and sprang up at Max. The slimy, toxic forepaws swiped at him, death glistening from every black-and-yellow finger.

But Max was too quick. He hadn't spent hours practicing on the basketball court for nothing. The frog was coming at him, just like the Green Park captain had, and this time he was ready.

He threw himself into a dodge, ducking one frog forefoot and twisting out of the way of the other all in one fluid move. Too bad Coach Baker wasn't here to see it!

The frog found itself grappling with nothing but air. It floundered for a moment on the crumbling ledge, confused.

A blinking orange light caught Max's eye. He looked up to where Glower was hovering. The firefly was flashing like a beacon, trying to get Max's attention. Then Max saw why. A huge, loose clump of dirt was hanging down from a tangle of roots directly above the frog.

If Max could knock it loose, he might be saved. His eyes flashed across the ground, looking for something to throw. He spotted a dry old acorn and snatched it up, just as the frog turned around with fury in its eyes.

Max got ready to take his shot. He was about to run closer, just to be sure, and then stopped. Coach Baker's words came back to him. *"Sometimes you gotta take a long shot . . ."*

He gripped the acorn, leaped, and threw.

The nut whacked the clump of earth. A thunderous rain of mud and gravel fell from the shaken roots. It completely buried the startled poison dart frog, until only one feebly waving arm could be seen.

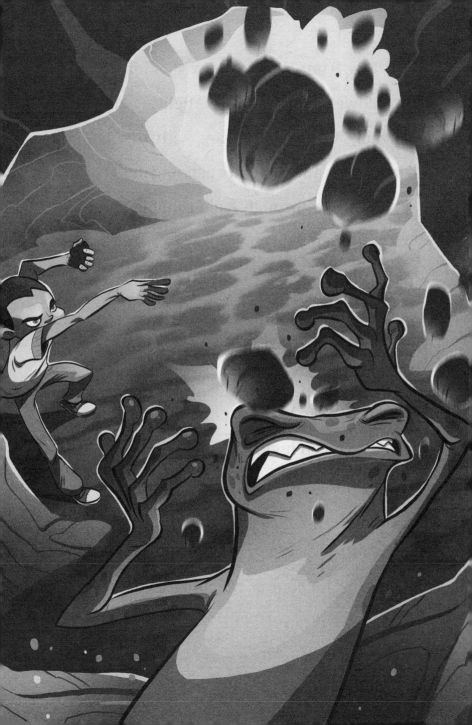

"Now's our chance," Max shouted. "Run!"

Glower shot past Max, lighting the way ahead. Max ran and ran, with the poison dart frog's angry shouts echoing in his ears.

They ran through wide tunnels and narrow tunnels, through flinty crevices and down sloping web-draped hallways, until Max staggered to an exhausted halt.

"I think we lost him," he said.

"Brilliant work," Glower said, settling down beside Max. "I can see why Barton values you so highly!"

"Thanks. Any idea where we are?"

"I think we've come full circle. If I'm not mistaken, the bug army should be right above us. Of course, reaching them may not be so easy."

"What about Lumens and Pulsar?" Max asked frantically.

Glower looked grave. "Lumens will help Pulsar. She's one of my best agents."

Max could only hope Glower was right. For now, though, they had to get aboveground. Luckily, it took the firefly only a few moments to discover a tunnel up to the surface. Soon after, they saw a narrow shaft of light blazing down and heard the familiar high-pitched *skree-skree-skree* of the cicada brigade.

"Between you and me, I'm tempted to stay down here," Glower admitted. "Those cicadas give me a headache!"

"Me, too. But we've got to find Barton."

"Agreed. Come on."

Max and Glower dug their way up, widening the tunnel exit until they were able to squeeze through and stagger out into the bright light. *I never want to go through anything like that again*, thought Max.

They'd emerged in the midst of the cicada troops, who were regrouping after the flycatcher attack. Max pushed his way through them angrily. "I need to find Barton!" he shouted. "Where is he?"

The cicadas ignored him. They seemed interested only in blasting out their high-pitched marching song. Max rolled his eyes and shoved past them.

Then, to his delight, a familiar droning sound came from above, growing louder.

"Max!" yelled Buzz, swooping in to land. "You're alive!"

"Just barely!" Max said. "We need to talk to Barton, right away."

"Consider it done. Climb aboard."

A short flight later, Max and Glower were reunited not only with Barton, but with Webster and Spike, too. They had all been frantically searching for him, fearing the worst after the flycatcher snatched him off Spike's back.

"I'm afraid the bird attack was devastating," Barton rumbled, hanging his huge head. "Our only option was to retreat, hide, and wait for them to leave."

"Hiding was my idea," Webster piped up.

"Hiding is *always* your idea, fraidybug," Spike said. "It just so happens it was the right idea. This time."

"I need your intelligence more than ever, Max," Barton said gravely. "The bugs will fight courageously if I give the order, but if they have to fight birds and lizards at the same time, they will undoubtedly lose."

"I don't back down from any fight!" Spike raged, flexing his stinger.

Barton sighed. "And what if it's a fight we can't win?"

Just then, Max had an idea. What was it the frog had said about the birds? *"The minute there's any real trouble, they get scared . . ."*

"Maybe fighting the birds is a mistake," he said.

Buzz gasped. "Max, you can't be suggesting we surrender!"

"I'm not." Max grinned. "But what if we don't have to *fight* them at all? Maybe we can do something else instead."

BATTLE BUGS ATTACK!

The noonday sun blazed down on the Pincer Plains. The bugs, back in marching formation, moved to the rhythm of the cicadas' screeching song. Max rode at the very front, on Spike's back, to meet the enemy.

On the Pincer Plains, the Lizard Army soon came into view. Max had never seen a force so large. The lizards and their amphibian allies were there by the hundreds. Max saw skinks, newts, snakes, iguanas, even chameleons and frilled lizards. It made his heart thump with fear.

But the bugs had an army of their own. The striding mantises looked ready to take on any threat. Behind them came rank after rank of venomous arthropods, from lethal centipedes to the sinister, stalking black widow spiders.

Up from the midst of the Lizard Army rose the massive head of General Komodo. "Where are you, Barton?" he bellowed. "Where are you hiding among all your scuttling friends?"

"I'm right here, Komodo," Barton shouted back from the bug ranks. "Losing your eyesight, are you? Maybe you're too old for this!"

"Joke while you can, insect," sneered General Komodo. "Now that we have the flycatchers on our side, you bugs don't stand a chance."

Max braced himself. Any minute now . . .

"Battle Bugs! Attack!" boomed Barton.

The front ranks of both armies charged at each other, sending up clouds of dust. Max clung tight to Spike, trying not to be jolted off. The scorpion made straight for a lizard platoon, yelling his battle cry. A group of smaller scorpions squeaked cries of their own and followed him into the fray.

Spike grabbed hold of the first lizard he could reach. As the reptile struggled in his

powerful pincers, he drove home his stinger.
The lizard's eyes bulged. "That's what you
get!" Spike growled. Other lizards moved
to surround him, hissing and striking at
him with their claws. One bit hard on his
forelimb, but couldn't break his thick
body armor. Max helpfully kicked it until it
let go.

"Thanks, shorty!" Spike said.

"We're a team, aren't we?" Max shouted
back.

He looked around for his other bug
friends. Buzz was leading a flying battalion
against the brightly colored poison dart
frogs. The hornets were ducking and weav-
ing, using their stingers to jab the frogs. The
frogs were hopping up and down, trying to

grab on to the hornets and coat them in their slimy poison.

Webster and his spider troops were goading the lizards into clever webbing traps, where they struggled and shrieked for help. On every side, the bugs were fighting for their homes . . . and their lives.

The battle raged back and forth. Bugs bit and stung; lizards gulped and snapped. Even through the chaos of fierce fighting, it was clear the bugs were starting to turn the tide. Not even the muscular iguanas could fight back against a horde of determined bugs that swarmed all over them and stung them into submission.

Finally, General Komodo let out a shrieking command: "We have waited long enough.

Now we end this! Vermilion flycatchers, ENGAGE!"

Max quickly looked up. The deadly little red birds were gathering in the sky, ready to swoop down from above.

Beneath him, Spike grunted, "Whatever you've got up your sleeve, little buddy, we could really use it about now!"

"Let's head back to the main forces, Spike. Double-time!"

Max wheeled Spike around and headed for the rear ranks of the bug army. He found the cicada battalion still playing their marching song for all they were worth.

"Ready, guys? Let's go!"

He led the cicadas right into the heart of the bug army. Spike shuddered. "I hope you know what you're doing. Cicadas can't fight for beans!"

"They don't need to," Max said, as the bird squadrons came closer and closer. They were doing a power dive. Good. That should make this work all the better.

"You might want to cover your ears, Spike," he said. "If you have any, that is."

"Eh?" said Spike, completely baffled.

"Incoming!" roared Barton, as the fly-catchers came swooping in for the kill.

Max turned to the cicadas. "Ready . . . three, two, one, NOW!"

As one, the cicadas blasted out a shriek so loud and high-pitched that Max thought his eardrums would burst. It sounded exactly like a sonic bird-scaring device he'd once heard on a visit to the city. Hopefully it would work just as well this time.

He covered his ears to block out the noise. Bugs and lizards alike stopped fighting and groaned in pain, writhing around at the terrible noise.

But the effect on the birds was astonishing. As if an invisible force had struck them, they rebounded backward into the air, wheeling and flapping chaotically. Their formation broke apart. Some of them, hurtling too fast to stop, spun out of control and slammed down onto the battlefield.

"Keep it up!" Max shouted to the cicadas. "It's working!"

In seconds, General Komodo's secret weapon was shattered. The flycatchers bolted from the field in complete disarray. Underneath their tough appearances, the flycatchers were cowards. A blast of screaming sound had broken their nerve completely.

"He's done it," said Barton, as he watched the last of the flycatchers vanish over the horizon. "Max has defeated the birds!"

MANTIS MOVES

General Komodo let out a roar of anger. "Come back, you feathered fools! We had a deal! Keep fighting!"

He might as well have been shouting at the clouds. The birds were gone.

"No matter," seethed the giant reptile. "Secret weapon or not, I can still defeat you. All troops, attack!"

"But, General," stammered a cowering chameleon, "the flycatchers were supposed to be our air support! Without them, the bugs might—"

"SILENCE!" With a whack of his huge tail, Komodo sent the chameleon flying into the battle. "When your general tells you to fight, you fight!"

Max rode up next to Barton. They watched the lizards attack, but it was clear there was no real battle plan. Only fear of Komodo was pushing them forward. This was the bugs' chance!

"Send in the mantises," Max urged Barton. "They can fly short distances, right? They can get right behind the lizards' lines and attack from behind."

"Yes! The mantises, of course. And with the flycatchers gone, there's nothing to stop them!"

Barton gave the order. The mantis brigades launched themselves into the air. They couldn't fly far, but they didn't have to.

The frightened lizards soldiers suddenly found they were surrounded. Mantises kept dropping out of the sky—*like paratroopers*, thought Max—and striking them with their strong claws before they could react.

Confusion spread through the lizard ranks. Many of the lizards couldn't see their commanding officers, let alone hear them, because of the sheer numbers of bugs rushing over them. One by one, aching from

stings, bites, and claw wounds, they gave up the fight and ran.

General Komodo looked to the left and right. His troops were running. Against all odds, the bugs had driven them back. His expression turned from disbelief to bitter resignation.

"Another time, Barton!" he hissed, turning his scaly back.

Then away he went, lumbering over the Pincer Plains toward the sea, his broken and wounded army trailing after him.

"I'll be waiting," Barton called. "As always."

"And so will I," Max said, patting Barton's gleaming carapace.

A cheer went up from the bug army, as the lizards retreated in disarray. The cicadas struck up their fighting song again, but this time, nobody complained. Those bugs had proved themselves beyond a shadow of a doubt.

As the lizards slithered off, Max saw a welcome sight emerge from the ground ahead of them: "Lumens and Pulsar!" he cried. Max had thought he would never see them again.

"Never leave a bug behind." Glower smiled triumphantly, as Lumens dragged Pulsar across the plains to safety.

Now that the danger was past, Max knew he had to leave, and so did the bugs. Webster,

Buzz, Spike, and Barton gathered to say good-bye. Glower came and joined them.

"We are all in your debt," Glower said.

"Your quick thinking has saved Bug Island once again," Barton added. "We will miss you, Max. I couldn't be prouder of you if you were my own grub."

Max laughed, imagining what his mom would think of that. "Bye for now, gang. I hope you won't need me *too* soon!"

He pulled the magnifying glass from his pocket and held it up to the sky. Immediately, powerful forces dragged him up, sucking him back through whirling, spiraling space until . . .

Thump. He landed flat on his back,

staring at the locker room ceiling back at Burgdale Elementary.

He picked himself up and dashed out of the locker room, praying the game wasn't over. The players were heading back onto the court. Coach Baker was yelling his name. He was just in time!

Max sprinted onto the court with a fast glance at the scoreboard: tied again, now at 34! With only twenty seconds left to play . . . and Green Park's ball! The whistle blew, and a Green Park player threw the ball in from the sidelines to his captain.

The Green Park captain quickly dribbled it down to the Burgdale hoop, with a smirk that said he considered the game as good as over. He wasn't prepared for Max to blind-side him and leap in at the last moment like a mantis, snatching the ball away.

"What the . . . who taught you *that* move?" the boy cried.

"You wouldn't believe me if I told you," said Max.

Then he was off, racing down to the other end of the court, to the Green Park hoop. A step, a leap—swish! Nothing but net!

The buzzer sounded. Coach Baker leaped to his feet. So did everyone in the bleachers. "That's the game!" the coach cheered, flinging his hat into the air. He strode past the openmouthed rival coach to join the crowd of players and fans who were lifting Max onto their shoulders.

Max caught a glimpse of the Green Park captain's scowling face. The boy stuck out his tongue. Just for a second, he looked a lot like a certain Komodo dragon Max knew all too well.

Max grinned. Victory was sweet—especially when you got a double helping!

REAL LIFE BATTLE BUGS!

Praying Mantis

Praying mantis is the common name for a whole order of insects called the Mantidea. They come in all sorts of different shapes and sizes, from the dead leaf mantis, which camouflages itself as a crisp, brown leaf, to the glass mantis, which is completely see-through.

But one thing they all have in common is the trait that gives them their name. The unusual angle of the praying mantis's front legs makes it seem like these insects are deep in prayer.

Mantises start off small, eating tiny flies and insects. However, as they get bigger and bigger, their appetites grow, too, and then nothing's off the menu. Mantises have been known to eat small lizards, scorpions, frogs, snakes, and even fish.

Cicada

The cicada is a fascinating and diverse species, with some groups known for their high-pitched "singing," and others for their epic hibernations.

The vast majority of cicadas' lives start underground, where they mature before emerging after a few months or years when they're ready. The periodical cicada is much more unusual. This insect emerges from the ground with the rest of its population at exactly the same time.

Since the cicadas can't communicate with one another underground, biologists are still baffled as to how they manage to surface at exactly the same time. However, some believe that the cicadas are able to use the tree roots they eat as they grow to determine the passage of time aboveground.

Once they do emerge, they behave like any other cicadas in the race to create the next generation. The males' "singing" is designed to attract females but also has the handy by-product of being able to deter predators. In fact, the noise is one of the loudest in the insect world!

THE ADVENTURE CONTINUES!

Turn the page for a Battle Bugs sneak peek!

Max Darwin shuffled down the driveway toward his mom's car, keeping his black cape wrapped tightly around him.

His mom looked at her watch, rolled her eyes, and opened the passenger door. "Hurry up, or we'll be late for the birthday party!"

"I'm coming!" Max protested, bunny-hopping the rest of the way and wriggling into the backseat. He could have moved a lot faster if he'd just let the cape go loose, but that would have ruined everything. Carefully, he set his backpack down beside him, not revealing the slightest glimpse of what might be inside his costume.

"I know you want to surprise Tyler, but I don't know why you can't let *me* see what you're wearing." His mom sighed, starting up the car and accelerating onto the road. "After all, you did raid my fabric stash to make it!"

"I'm pupating," Max insisted, as if that explained everything.

"Oh, right," his mom continued. "So, you can't come out of your cocoon too soon?"

"Exactly!" Max grinned, jiggling with excitement, as his mom drove them through the streets toward Tyler's house. He already knew what his best friend would be dressed as. Tyler was just as obsessed with super-heroes as Max was with bugs. But Max's costume had been a closely guarded secret so far.

"How about I guess?" his mom suggested.

Max just groaned—she'd never be able to figure it out.

"Let's see. A pretty butterfly?"

"Nope," Max said.

"Hmm. Maybe . . . a moth?"

"Wrong again."

"Something nastier? A wasp?"

Max laughed. "No. You'll just have to wait!"

"Fine, fine, you win. I give up." His mom laughed. "Now, where are we? Furze Avenue . . . oh. Oh, no!"

Max sat bolt upright. "What's wrong, Mom?"

"Tyler's present!" she wailed. "I don't remember putting it in the car. Last time I saw it, it was on the kitchen table! We need to turn the car around . . ."

"Wait!" Max called, already rummaging inside his backpack. He pulled out the long, gift-wrapped package—a light-up power sword he'd chosen for Tyler himself.

"Got it!" he shouted. "It's right here."

"Phew," his mom said. "Crisis averted. It's a good thing one of us has their head screwed on right!"

While he had his backpack open, Max felt inside for the huge, heavy shape of his *Encyclopedia of Arthropods*. Sure enough, the book was in there, along with the magnifying glass that went with it. Ever since his mom had brought it back from an estate auction, the book had never been far from Max's side.

The mysterious old book was not only full of bugs of all different types that Max could look up, it was also full of a strange magic, capable of transporting Max to an amazing world of talking bugs. He'd already had adventures on Bug Island, and the bugs could call him back at a moment's notice.

His mom glanced back at him and groaned. "Do you have to bring that dusty old encyclopedia everywhere you go?"

"Of course," Max said. "Bugs are everywhere!"

"Sometimes I worry you might turn into a bug overnight," his mom joked.

Max couldn't think of anything cooler!